Danny Longlegs

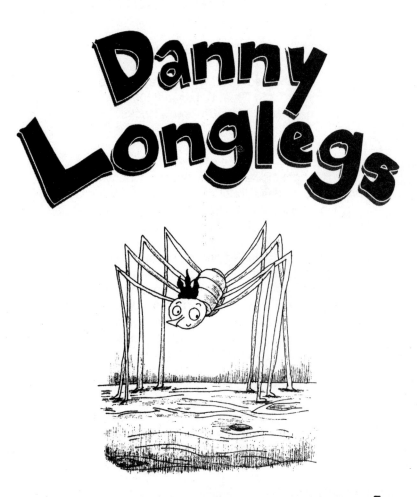

Damon Burnard

For the Little Bugs - Cindy,
Wally and Lilly

Published as a My First Read Alone
in Great Britain in 2000
by Hodder Children's Books

10 9 8 7 6 5 4 3 2 1

ISBN 0 340 78781 3

Printed and bound by Omnia Books Ltd, Glasgow

Hodder Children's Books
a division of Hodder Headline Limited
338 Euston Road
London NW1 3BH

Visit Damon's website!
http://home1.gte.net/dburnard

Danny Longlegs lived by an old garden shed.

Can you find him?

Here's a clue: look on the rake!

This is Danny, close up.

As you can see, he had very
long legs. Danny was VERY tall.

Sometimes Danny liked being tall.

He could see over long grass . . .

. . . and wade through puddles.

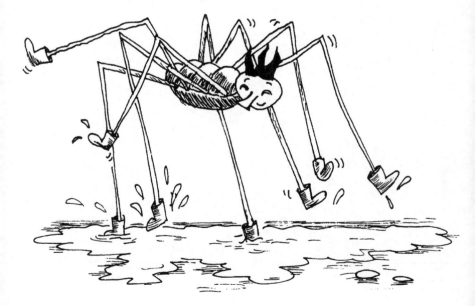

But being tall wasn't always fun.

Playing hide-and-seek was hard . . .

. . . and sometimes he felt left out.

Worst of all, it was hard for Danny
to do his favourite thing.

Can you guess what that was?

Danny's favourite thing was
football!

Every day Danny played football
on the roof of the shed . . .

But being so tall was a problem.

The ball kept rolling through
his legs . . .

. . . and sometimes, when Danny
tried to kick it . . .

. . . he got all tangled up!

Danny hated that. And he hated
it when the other bugs made fun
of him.

Mikey Mite was the worst.
He was always picking on Danny.

'Ha ha!' he laughed.

'It's not funny, Mikey!' said Danny.
'Stop it!'

'No, I won't!' said Mikey. 'It's my
ball!'

But not everyone was mean like Mikey.

'Don't listen to him!' said Rocky Roach.

'Thanks, Rocky!' said Danny.

But though he played EVERY day, he didn't get much better.

One Monday, Danny walked up
to the roof of the shed.

'Can I play?' he asked.

But Mikey didn't agree.

'We need to practise for Friday!'
he snapped.

'Friday?' asked Danny.

'We're playing Cabbage Patch United,' said Mikey's friend, Slimo. 'We haven't beaten them for years!'

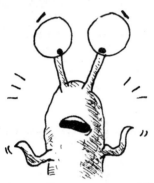

'Can I be on the team?' asked Danny.

'No way!' Mikey Laughed.

'Go on, give him a chance!' said
Rocky.
'Nope!' said Mikey.

Mikey and Slimo stomped off.

'Sorry, Danny!' said Rocky.
'Maybe he'll change his mind
tomorrow!'
'Maybe,' said Danny.

He sat down to watch, instead.

On Tuesday, Danny asked Mikey again.

'NO!' said Mikey.

So Danny had to watch, again.

On Wednesday, Danny tried once more.

'NO!' said Mikey.

Danny sighed. It was hopeless.

He decided to go.

On his way back home . . .

. . . Danny saw a bug he'd never met before.

Hello,' he said.

'I'm Erika Earwig,' said the bug. 'I've just moved here, and I don't like it one bit!'

'I want to play football,' she grumbled. 'But Mikey Mite won't let me.'

Why not?

'Because I'm a GIRL!' said Erika. 'That's not fair!' said Danny. And he sighed.

'Hey, what's wrong with you?' asked Erika.

'That's not fair!' said Erika. 'Then how can you get better?'

And then she had an idea.

'Alright!' said Danny.

Together they crawled off the shed . . .

. . . and found a place to play.

Erika juggled the ball from foot
to foot . . .

. . . flicked it into the air . . .

. . . and kicked it to Danny.

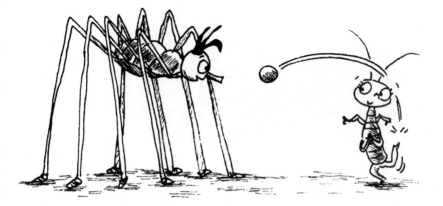

'You're good!' said Danny.
'Thanks!' Erika smiled. 'Now,
I'll be in goal.'

'OK!' said Danny.

But as he kicked the ball . . .

. . . he slipped!

'Mikey's right!' he groaned. 'I'm useless!'

Suddenly . . .

THEN . . .

The ball bounced off his head . . .

. . . and flew past Erika!

'WOW!' Danny shouted.

'Ha ha!' Erika laughed. 'Do that again, Danny!'

Danny and Erika practised for hours that day . . .

. . . and all of the next day, too.

And then came Friday. The day of the big match.

A large crowd waited on a rhubarb leaf . . .

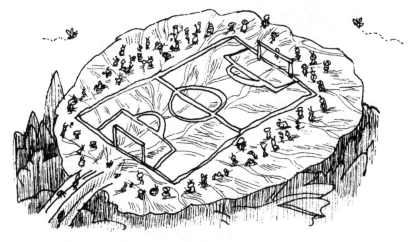

Danny and Erika sat down next to Grandpa Beetle.

Out ran the teams . . .

. . . the ref blew his whistle . . .

. . . and the game began.

Cabbage Patch United were mean.
They hid the ref's glasses . . .

. . . and they tripped and pushed
the Shed Bugs.

But the Shed Bugs still scored
first!

Cabbage Patch United got even
meaner . . .

And then . . .

. . . they scored, too!

With a minute left to play, the teams had one goal each.

Mikey had the ball . . .

Suddenly . . .

The ball rolled to Rocky and . . .

'Come on, ref!' shouted Erika and
Danny.

But the referee was still looking for
his glasses!

Mikey and Rocky left the pitch . . .

'Me and Erika could stand in for you!' said Danny.

'Are you crazy?' groaned Mikey. 'Don't worry,' said Danny. 'We won't let you down. Come on Erika!'

Cabbage Patch United had first
kick . . .

Erika won it . . .

. . . and ran.

Danny ran, too.

'Ha ha!' laughed Cabbage Patch
United.

But Danny wasn't listening.
'Now, Erika!' he shouted.

Erika kicked the ball high into the air . . .

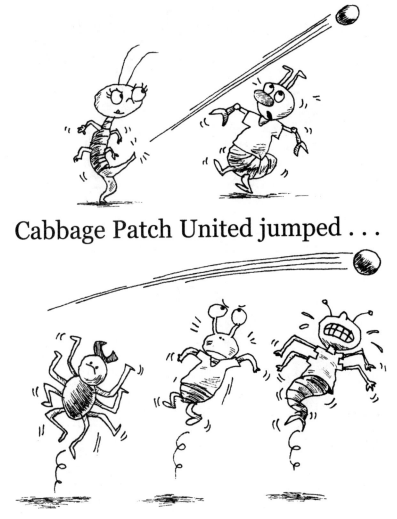

Cabbage Patch United jumped . . .

. . . but they just couldn't reach it!

Danny kept his eyes on the ball . . .

. . . and THEN . . .

Into the goal it flew!

'GOAL!' shouted Danny and
Erika.

'YAHOO!' cheered the Shed Bugs.

And then . . .

The game was over!

'We did it!' yelled Rocky.

'Well done, Danny!' said Grandpa Beetle. 'We haven't beaten Cabbage Patch United since I was a boy!'

He gave Danny a football of his very own.

The Shed Bugs had a big party!

'Let's hear it for Danny and
Erika!' shouted Rocky.

'Thanks, Erika!' said Danny.
'No, thank YOU, Danny!' said
Erika.

After the party, Danny picked up his football.

'Anyone fancy a game?' he asked. 'Yeah!' shouted the Shed Bugs.

. . . all except for Mikey.

'Hey . . . Danny,' he said quietly.

The other bugs looked at Danny.

Danny smiled.

'Of course!' he said. 'Everyone can play!'

So the bugs played all together,
under the silver moon . . .

Afterwards they made up a new
rule . . .

Tall or short, narrow or wide,
girl or boy, everyone was welcome
to play.

It was fairer that way . . .

. . . and much more fun!